For my grandchildren: Leah, Samuel, Hannah, Ian, Aidan, and Riley —M. H. W.

to Daniel, Leslie, Enzo, Zelda, and Johanna in Tensta —R. G. C.

Text © 2008 by Muriel Harris Weinstein.
Illustrations © 2008 by R. Gregory Christie.

Book design by Sara Gillingham.
The illustrations for this book were rendered in acrylic.
Manufactured in China.

Library of Congress Cataloging-in-Publication Data
Weinstein, Muriel Harris.
When Louis Armstrong taught me scat / by Muriel Harris Weinstein ;
illustrated by R. Gregory Christie.
p. cm.
Summary: After dancing to music on the radio before she goes to bed,
a young girl learns how to sing scat when Louis Armstrong comes to her in a dream.
Includes facts about Louis Armstrong and scat singing.
ISBN 978-0-8118-5131-2
1. Armstrong, Louis, 1901–1971–Juvenile fiction.
[1. Armstrong, Louis, 1901–1971–Fiction. 2. Jazz–Fiction. 3. Singing–Fiction.
4. African Americans–Fiction.] I. Christie, Gregory, 1971– ill. II. Title.
PZ7.W43669Wh 2008
[E]–dc22
2007044305

10 9 8 7 6 5 4 3 2 1

Chronicle Books
680 Second Street, San Francisco, California 94107

www.chroniclekids.com

WHEN Louis Armstrong TAUGHT ME Scat

chronicle books · san francisco

BY MURIEL HARRIS WEINSTEIN ILLUSTRATED BY R. GREGORY CHRISTIE

Music ripples out of our table radio. Momma kicks back her chair and grabs my hands. "Let's dance, Sugar," she says. "Can't waste good music."

I love dancing with Momma. We spin an' twirl around, waggle our heads an' wiggle our hips, and our backsides bobble like balloons. My mouth chews Double Bubble and my legs fly. The swingy music jumps inside my body, rolls riffs on my tongue, and tootles to my toes.

"That Louis sure can sing," Momma says, singing along with him. **"Doo-blee-ooo-doo."**

"What kind of words are those?" I ask.

"Scat," says Momma.

"Scat? What's THAT?"

"It's sounds you make up," says Momma, swinging me out.

"Doo-blee-OOO-DOO.

Try it. Fly it. Fly it like a kite, Sugar."

"I'll sing it. String it. String it out like beads," I tell her, spinning like a record. **"Doo-blee-OOO-DOO."**

When the music stops, I don't want to.

"DOOBIE-OOOBIE-DOOO-BOOO."

Before long the hands of the clock point to bedtime. Slipping under my blanket, scat words flash through my brain in neon, jump like Bo Peep's sheep, and I follow them to sleep.

A horn is blowing, throwing long shadows on my walls. I love its **wah-wah-wah-ing** sound.

It stops and a deep, gravelly voice sings out,

"HEY, YOU WANNA SCAT?
Scat like a *purring cat?*"

I know that voice.

It's Louis Armstrong!

to sing *scat,"*

Louis sings.

"But I'm only a beginner," I say.

"That's OK. Just follow me.

Dooo-bleee-ooo-DIP-DOP."

"Dooo-bleee-ooo-DIP-DOP," I sing.

"Pretty gooooood. Now whaddya wanna scat about?"
sweet Louis asks.

"How about bubble gum?"

"Sure. Bubble gum's hip."

Louis thinks a minute and sings:

oooba lee COOOO, oooba lee CAT
bubble me a bubble
an' bubble it FAT.

oooba lee COOOO,
oooba lee BAT

blow me a bubble in
bubble gum SCAT.

RIPPETY wrapper
glittery new
PINKETY SWEET
stickety CHEW

SQUASH-ITEE
stretch-itee
gummity thick

SQUOOZ-ITEE
oooz-itee
blowitty quick!

OOOO-blee BOOO-blee JIPPITTY JOON
WOBBLY BUBBLE'S a lilac moon
BUTTERFLY'S COCOON
BABOON'S nose

hippo's toes

OOOO-blee BOOO-blee
slippetty
spun

WOBBLY BUBBLE'S
a roseee sun
gummy bun

lolly pop
PARACHUTE DROP!!!

CRICKET'S THRONE

puppy's bone

bug's umbrella

mozzarella???

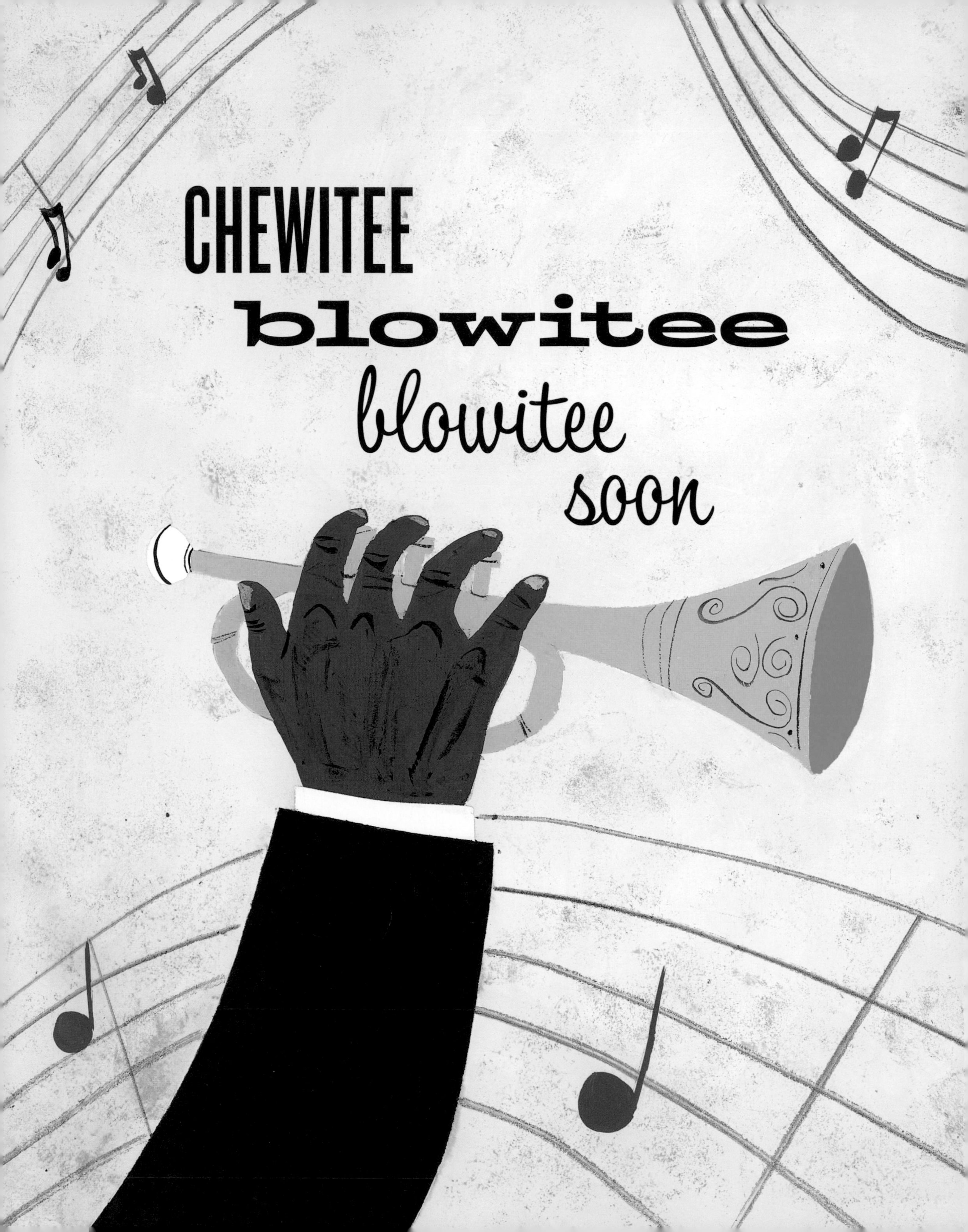

The next morning I scat looking in the mirror. And I scat unfrizzing my hair. And I scat eating cereal. And I scat down the stairs. And when I run outdoors, the kids are jamming to Double Dutch jump, and I leap in and scat my scat song. And in seconds the whole neighborhood is jumping and scatting my (and Louis's) bubble gum song.

oooba lee COOOO,
oooba lee CAT

bubble me a bubble
an' **bubble it FAT.**

oooba lee COOOO,
oooba lee BAT

BLOW ME A BUBBLE IN
bubble gum scat.

A FEW WORDS ABOUT
Louis Armstrong

August 4, 1901—July 6, 1971

Louis Armstrong grew up in the poorest neighborhood in New Orleans, and he always had to have odd jobs to help make extra money for his family. But no matter how difficult the job, Louis never complained. He had the kind of personality that always found something to be happy about. And the joy that bubbled up inside of him also bubbled in his music. Everyone who knew Louis loved him. He had a smile so wide, his friends said it was as big as an open satchel. So they nicknamed him "Satchmo." Years later, after he had become famous and had played for kings and queens and presidents all around the world, he was dubbed "Satchmo the Ambassador," because his music brought so much goodwill to the world.

Louis Armstrong was one of the world's greatest jazz trumpeters. He wrote music, he wrote the lyrics, and he loved to perform. His music was so contagious that when he played, people just had to sway, or clap, or wiggle their hips.

Musicians he played with tried to copy Louis's style and the way he played, but it was not an easy thing to do. Louis held his notes for a long time and not all musicians can do that. He held on so long that you could almost hear his notes in the air after he stopped blowing them.

Louis Armstrong was born in New Orleans on August 4, 1901, but he loved the United States so much, he decided to celebrate his birthday on July 4. He died on July 6, 1971.

A FEW WORDS ABOUT

Scat

"Scat" is singing nonsense words, sounds, or syllables instead of lyrics. Although there are recordings of West African tribes creating sounds similar to scat, before Louis Armstrong, no one sang it professionally. He loved it, even as a kid. For example, he might sing "ooblee-oo-la-dee, doo-wah-bloo" instead of actual words. It was fun.

Some vocalists liked it so much that they imitated Louis. Ella Fitzgerald, Sarah Vaughan, and Mel Tormé all sang scat. But Louis was the first to sing it and the first to make a record singing scat. That record was called *Heebie Jeebies,* and it was a solid hit. Though Louis Armstrong died in 1971, you can still hear him sing scat today on recordings.